Beast Quest®

DIPROX
THE BUZZING TERROR

BY ADAM BLADE

ORCHARD

With special thanks to Tabitha Jones

www.beastquest.co.uk

ORCHARD BOOKS

First published in Great Britain in 2020 by The Watts Publishing Group

1 3 5 7 9 10 8 6 4 2

Text © Beast Quest Limited 2020
Cover and inside illustrations by Steve Sims
© Beast Quest Limited 2020

Beast Quest is a registered trademark of Beast Quest Limited
Series created by Beast Quest Limited, London

A CIP catalogue record for this book is available from the British Library.

ISBN 978 1 40836 190 0

Printed in Great Britain

The paper and board used in this book are made from wood from responsible sources

Orchard Books
An imprint of Hachette Children's Group
Part of The Watts Publishing Group Limited
Carmelite House, 50 Victoria Embankment, London EC4Y 0DZ

An Hachette UK Company
www.hachette.co.uk
www.hachettechildrens.co.uk

Welcome to the world of Beast Quest!

Tom was once an ordinary village boy, until he travelled to the City, met King Hugo and discovered his destiny. Now he is the Master of the Beasts, sworn to defend Avantia and its people against Evil. Tom draws on the might of the magical Golden Armour, and is protected by powerful tokens granted to him by the Good Beasts of Avantia. Together with his loyal companion Elenna, Tom is always ready to visit new lands and tackle the enemies of the realm.

While there's blood in his veins, Tom will never give up the Quest...

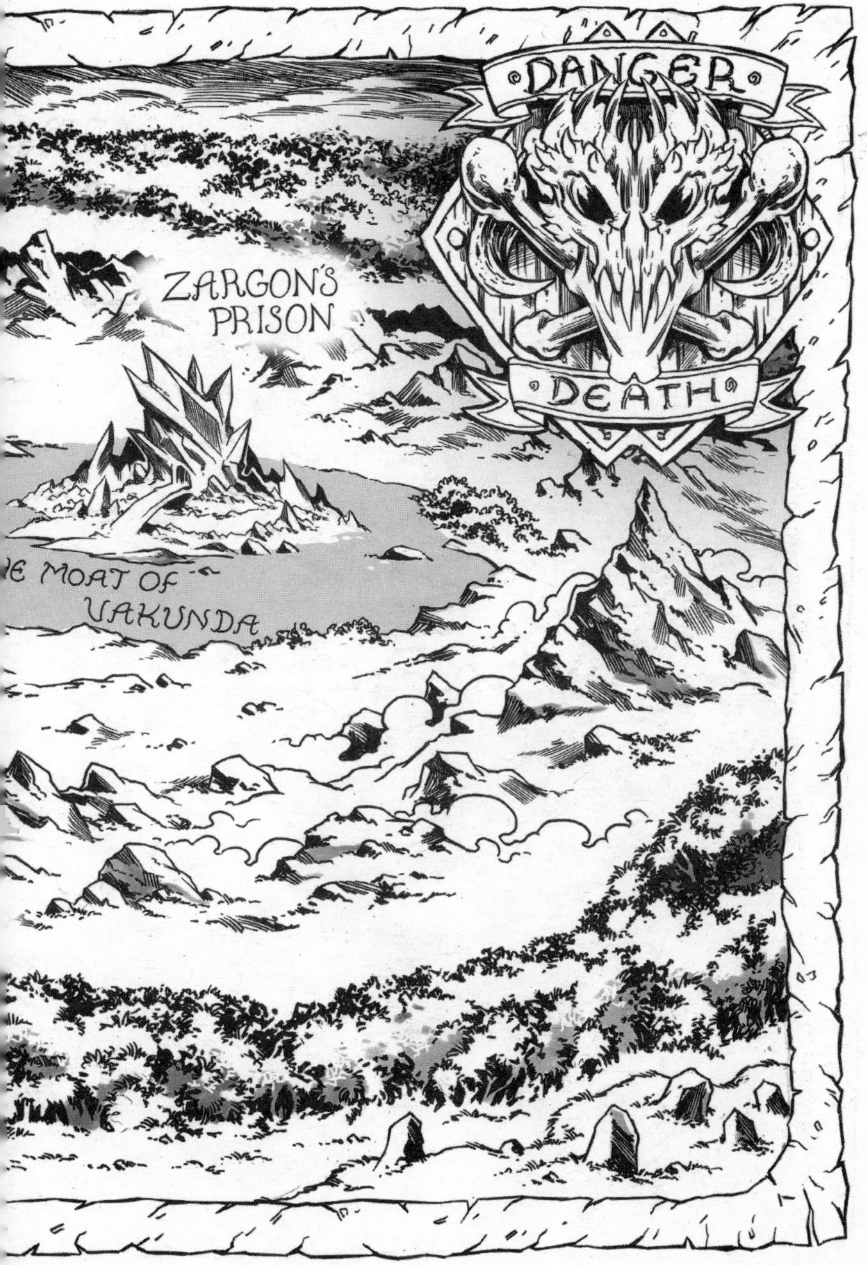
DANGER
DEATH
ZARGON'S PRISON
E MOAT OF VAKUNDA

There are special gold coins to collect in this book. You will earn one coin for every chapter you read.

Find out what to do with your coins at the end of the book.

CONTENTS

1. OUTCASTS   11

2. SANDSTORM!   23

3. QUICKSAND   39

4. A CRYSTAL ARMY   59

5. A CRYSTAL COFFIN   75

6. AROHA'S ANGUISH   87

7. DIPROX'S REVENGE   99

8. JUST REWARDS   117

When my aunt Aroha left Tangala to marry King Hugo of Avantia, I thought I could rule this kingdom. I wanted to make her proud, to protect the country's borders and keep my people safe.

I have failed. The sorcerer who took me claims to be hundreds of years old. He says he will not kill me, if my aunt does the right thing. It's the Jewels of Tangala that he wants. A simple swap – me for the magical stones. But if Aroha delivers them, the results will be far worse than one death. All Tangala will be in peril. My only hope is that my aunt has some other plan, some way to rescue me, but save the kingdom too.

She will need brave heroes at her side if she is to succeed.

Rotu
Regent of Tangala, and nephew to the queen.

OUTCASTS

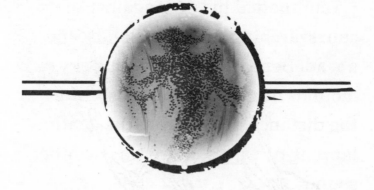

Tom waded out of the cool, clear water of the Crystal Sea and up on to its shingle beach. His boots squelched and his jerkin clung to his skin. Beside him, Elenna shook a rain of glittering droplets from her hair.

She glanced around. "I can't see any sign of Yara or the queen,"

Elenna said, her voice tight with worry.

Tom shaded his eyes against the sun, searching the bleak landscape ahead. Beneath the deep blue sky, mounds of pebbles stretched into the distance. Apart from the gentle lapping of waves, there was no other sound.

Tom sighed. "They can't be that far ahead of us."

"At least we know where they're going," Elenna said.

Tom nodded, remembering how the Crystal Sea formed a ring around the island. "Zargon's palace must be straight on. Let's go."

After filling their water bottles,

they set off, jogging over the shingle beach. Tom kept his eyes on the horizon, watching for any sign of Queen Aroha, or a Beast. Since they had arrived in Zargon's enchanted Kingdom of Vakunda in search of the queen's kidnapped nephew, they had already defeated three fearsome enemies. Tom knew one final Beast still awaited them, along with the Evil Wizard himself. Worry gnawed at his gut. He hated to think of Aroha facing such deadly foes without him and Elenna.

"I still can't understand why the queen would take Yara's side against us," he said. "It makes no sense – we've risked our lives again and again on this Quest. All Yara's done is get in the way, or worse. Aroha's no fool. What's got into her?"

"Perhaps she's still affected by those poisonous fungi that made us all fight each other," said Elenna. "Or maybe she can't believe that someone who has guarded her nephew for so long would betray her."

Tom remembered the look of fury on the queen's face when she ordered him and Elenna to abandon the Quest. "Either way," he said, "it's still down to us to protect her, and the jewels."

Zargon had demanded the Jewels of Tangala as a ransom for the prince. Even before Tom had seen the power of the gemstones at work, he knew that letting them fall into the wrong hands would be disastrous. Seeing how they could absorb the energy of defeated Beasts, and transform entire landscapes for the better, he was more determined than ever to keep them safe.

They reached the top of a crest in the land, and Tom saw that the shingle beach gave way to sand dunes baking under the sun. Elenna pointed to two sets of footprints leading into the distance, and they set off, jogging as fast as they could; but the powdery sand shifted with every step, making running exhausting.

The sun blazed down, and Tom soon
felt parched, but he forced himself
onwards. Each time he reached the
top of a new dune, he hoped to catch
sight of Aroha, or of Zargon's palace,
but all there was to see was the

barren sand stretching on and on, shimmering in a dazzling heat haze.

Finally, dizzy with thirst, Tom drew to a halt before a wide, flat stretch of desert. "Surely we have to be close to catching them," he panted.

"I hope so!" Elenna said, leaning her hands on her knees to get her breath. After taking a long drink of water, Tom called on the power of his enchanted helmet, part of his Golden Armour. The full suit was back in Avantia, but Tom was still able to draw on its magic to allow him to see across great distances. He could just make out two tiny figures. Beyond them, there was a line of something that glittered even more than the desert mirages.

"They're still a long way off!" Tom told Elenna.

"Then we'd better keep going," Elenna said, grimly. The sun climbed higher as they ran, the only sound the rasp of their breath in the hot, dry air. Tom's throat felt raw and his chapped lips were cracked and bleeding. But he could see the queen's glinting form, gradually drawing closer. *We're gaining on them!*

As Tom watched, a long low howl of wind whipped up eddies of sand in the distance, hiding Aroha from view. A gust rippled towards them over the desert, throwing dust into Tom's face. Narrowing his eyes, he saw what looked like a dense brown cloud of smoke, rolling towards them. His heart lurched.

"Sandstorm!" Elenna cried, her words almost drowned out by the wind. Tom clenched his jaw, his eyes

fixed on a strange, dark patch near
the heart of the sand cloud.

There's something in there, Tom

thought, lifting his shield.

"Elenna…I don't think this is a natural storm!"

SANDSTORM!

The sand cloud slammed into them, plunging them into half-darkness. The screeching wind snatched at Tom's body, threatening to tear his shield from his grip. Leaning into the wind with his eyes closed and his legs braced, he called on the magical strength of his golden breastplate.

"I can't hold on much longer!"

Elenna shouted, as she clung on to him to keep from being whisked away by the ferocious wind.

*I'm not sure I can, either...*Tom thought, every muscle strained. "Whoa!" He suddenly toppled

forwards, landing on his hands
and knees. He raised his head and
blinked his eyes open. As quickly
as it had arrived, the wind had
suddenly gone! Elenna slumped on
top of him. They both scrambled
up and turned to see the vast cloud
of sand sweeping across the desert,
away from them…

…until it stopped dead, sucking
up more sand into a huge spinning
vortex as it hung there, almost as
though it was considering which way
it was going to charge.

Then it hurtled back towards
them!

Tom knew they couldn't possibly
survive another encounter with the

moving wall of sand. There was nothing for it...

"Run!" Tom cried, grabbing Elenna's hand and leading her in a sprint. From close behind, he could hear the howl of the wind, gaining fast. He pushed himself to run faster, harder... The wind swept past on one side, the dark funnel of whirling dust turning around to block their path.

Something in the churning darkness caught Tom's eye. A huge muscular arm...a fist...a broad chest...a sneering, bearded face. He was massive, almost twice Tom's height. A furious enemy, made of swirling sand.

"Zargon!" Tom gasped, the outline

of the man growing clear.

The wizard's lips spread into a broad, mocking smile, his voice a hideous rasp. "That's right... Did you really think you could stop me? I am far too powerful, even without the Jewels of Tangala...and when I get my hands on them, I will be invincible!"

Tom stopped running, Elenna pausing beside him. He held the wizard's scornful gaze and drew his sword. "We've already defeated three of your Beasts," Tom called back. "I don't see why the last one should be any different. And while there's blood in my veins, I will keep the jewels out of your hands."

The sand wizard narrowed his eyes. His smile curled with hate. "Then I'll just have to use my hands to squeeze all the blood *out* of your veins, won't I?" he roared.

"No! Tom, watch out!" But Elenna's warning came too late. Zargon's sandy outline blurred as he swept forwards, slamming a massive balled fist into Tom's stomach.

"Oof!" The air exploded from Tom's lungs as his feet left the ground. He landed hard on his back and rolled over, gasping. Looking up through watering eyes, Tom saw Elenna fire an arrow at Zargon's broad chest.

Twang! But Zargon's form swirled, disappearing in a column of sand.

The arrow sailed straight through
without leaving a mark as Elenna
watched, open-mouthed.

The clouds of sand raced together to quickly re-form Zargon's figure. He reached Elenna in two quick paces, lifted his hand, and dashed her aside. As Elenna fell sprawling to the ground, Zargon turned back to Tom, eyes blazing with hate.

"When will you give up?" Zargon asked.

Tom spat the grit from between his teeth. "Never!" he cried, doing his best to sound defiant even though his mind was reeling. *How can we fight sand and wind?* Beyond Zargon, Elenna lay motionless, her limbs spread awkwardly. Tom felt a stab of alarm, but then he saw her open first one eye, then the other.

She raised her brows meaningfully at him, and glanced towards her water bottle, which now lay beside her, thrown free from her belt.

Tom frowned in confusion. But, with Zargon's back still to her, Elenna drew her finger across her throat and tipped her head towards her bottle. Tom had to stifle a grin as he understood. *Good thinking... But I'll need to distract Zargon for Elenna's plan to work...*

Tom lifted his sword once more and raised his eyes to the towering figure of sand. As Zargon sneered down at him, Tom swallowed hard, taking one step backwards...then another, lowering his blade, letting his hand shake. For the first time in his life, he was allowing himself to look like a coward.

"Ha! I knew you'd surrender!" Zargon spat. "But don't think I'll let you escape!" The wizard drew back his mighty fist. Calling on the magical speed of his golden leg armour, Tom dodged sideways and sprinted away. They had to be quick. Soon, Zargon would notice that Elenna wasn't moving, and he might go to investigate.

Glancing back, he saw the wizard's tall figure dissolve into a tornado once more, then hurtle towards him faster than ever. *He's falling for it!* Tom sped on, cutting away from Elenna, then back towards her. He slowed his pace and allowed the spinning vortex to gain on him. The sand was difficult to run across, so it wasn't hard at all to slow down!

As Zargon's whirlwind closed in behind him, Tom heard the roar of evil laughter. Tom drew near to Elenna's body, making his breath noisy and ragged. Finally, he stopped and bent double, then dropped to his knees, gasping. The tornado slowed as it approached him, Zargon's triumphant laughter sounding on the air as the sand re-took the wizard's form.

Don't laugh too soon, thought Tom. It took all of his willpower not to leap up and wipe the smirk off the wizard's face. But, no – they had to see Elenna's plan through!

Zargon lunged for Tom's throat…

Elenna shot to her feet. In one quick movement, she hurled the contents of her upturned bottle. Glittering water arced beneath the sun and landed in a spray over the back of Zargon's neck. *Perfect!* Tom watched as the sand turned dark and solid, shrinking into solid form.

"Now, Tom!" cried Elenna.

Tom sprang up, swinging his sword towards the wet sand. *Thwack!* Tom felt resistance beneath his blade – at last! It sliced through Zargon's neck, the sand peeling apart. Zargon gave a strangled gurgle and a groan

of protest, before his mighty head tumbled forwards, landing with a soft thud in the sand.

Instantly, the rest of his body toppled and broke apart. His fallen head began crumbling. But before it lost its form completely, the wizard's sneering lips parted. "Soon we will meet in the flesh," he said, his voice a dry, rasping hiss that sent a shiver down Tom's spine. "Then you will *really* suffer…"

QUICKSAND

Tom let out a shaky breath.

"Great plan, Elenna," he said. "But we haven't seen the last of Zargon. We'd better go. Yara and the queen will be even further ahead of us by now."

Gazing towards the glimmering line on the horizon, Tom called again on the magic of his golden helmet. The picture swam into focus. The desert was fringed by a forest, but instead of green leaves and brown bark, the trees shimmered like crystals. Bright sunlight glanced off the shining foliage, making Tom's eyes smart. He blinked the vision away.

"There's some sort of enchanted forest ahead," he told Elenna. "It looks like it's made of glass or crystal. Aroha and Yara must be inside."

As Tom and Elenna jogged closer to the glimmering treeline, Elenna gasped.

"It's amazing," she said.

Tom nodded. The three realms of

Vakunda they had passed through so far had been cursed and treacherous. But each time they had vanquished the region's Beast, the landscape had returned to a paradise. Zargon had created these realms five hundred years before, using the Jewels of Tangala. He'd meant them to be beautiful, not dangerous.

Tom's glance passed over the graceful crystal trees, their branches arcing like fingers of ice. He noticed at once that there were no birds or animals. Not a sound, other than the hiss of a breeze that made the crystal leaves dance and jangle like charms. Just like Vakunda's other cursed realms, the forest was dead.

Despite the heat, Tom suppressed a shiver. "It is beautiful," he said, "but that doesn't mean it's not dangerous. And there is still one more Beast to defeat. We'll need to stay focused."

As Tom stepped into the forest, blades of crystal grass exploded into sparkling powder under his boots. The light beneath the trees shifted in a dazzling kaleidoscope of colours, and the sun beat down through shards of glass to scorch Tom's back. It was almost impossible to keep his bearings – every piece of undergrowth shone crystal-bright, all looking exactly the same. Off at a small distance, Elenna weaved her way through the brilliant plants, careful to avoid the sharp points of glassy leaves.

"It's like a forest of diamond daggers!" she called.

Thankfully, the crystal thicket didn't stretch far. Tom was glad to emerge on the other side, stepping back out into blazing daylight. He blinked and shielded his eyes. Up ahead was an immense fortress, made of the same glinting crystal as the forest. A moat of sand surrounded the castle, spanned by a crystal drawbridge that gave off rainbow flashes as it lifted. Tom caught a glimpse of two figures beyond the closing gate. *Aroha and Yara!* Between them, they were raising the bridge with a glittering pulley.

"Wait!" Tom shouted. "Lower the

bridge! You'll need our help to defeat the last Beast!" But neither Yara nor the queen even looked in their direction.

Tom let out a growl of frustration as the gate closed smoothly. "Aroha loves her nephew… Why won't she let us help?"

Elenna frowned. "Maybe she really believes we'd just get in the way," she said. "We'll have to find another entrance." She glanced towards the castle. "At least the moat can't be shark-infested. It's full of sand."

"Hmmm," Tom said. "A sandy moat? I have a bad feeling about that." He turned and snapped a long, crystal branch from one of the sparkling trees. Then he stepped to the edge of the wide moat, and dropped it in. The surface of the sand looked solid, but the branch sank almost instantly, bubbles of gassy air rising up as it left no trace.

"Quicksand," Elenna said. She let out a sigh. "Of course. So, how do we get across?"

Tom looked at the smooth, sheer walls rising from the moat. "I could jump using the power of my golden boots," he said, "but I don't see anything to cling to. Let's see if there's another gate, or even a low window."

Tom led the way around the towering glass fortress, running his eyes up and down its shiny walls. The windows were only arrow slits, and all were too high to reach by jumping.

"We've come so far," Tom said, balling his fists. "There has to be a way in!"

"What about that?" Elenna asked, pointing to the castle wall, right at the point where it met the moat. "Is that an air vent? Or some sort of drainage channel?" Narrowing his eyes against the glare, Tom could make out what appeared to be a crystal grille covering an opening buried in the sand. It looked like it might just be wide enough for them to crawl through.

"It could be a way in," he said. "But it'll be dangerous." He thought of the queen, already inside Zargon's prison with no one but Yara to protect her.

"We'll have to risk it," he said. "I'll link us together with our rope and jump across, using my golden boots. The rope won't reach all the way, so we'll both have to leap as far as we can. Once I'm over, I'll grab the grate and pull you the rest of the way. Then I'll break the glass so we can get inside."

They each tied one end of the rope about their waists. Then, Tom and Elenna stood near the edge of the moat.

"Ready?" Tom asked.

"As ready as I'll ever be," Elenna said. "On the count of three?"

Tom nodded. "One…two…*three*!"

They both took running steps

towards the moat, then leapt as far as they could. As the shining wall drew close, Tom felt the rope tighten, but the magic of his golden boots carried him on, tugging Elenna behind him. As he landed near the glass vent, he threw his limbs wide to spread his weight. Instantly, he felt the dry, powdery sand shift beneath him. He was sinking already. Reaching for the grate, Tom tried to catch hold of it, but the grille was too narrow. He couldn't get his fingers through the holes.

"Hurry!" Elenna cried.

Tom glanced back to see that she was already up to her waist.

"Stay as still as possible!" Tom

told her. Then, calling on the strength of his golden breastplate, he slammed his fist hard into the grille. The crystal mesh didn't so much as crack. Fear rising inside him, he hit the grate again and again.

"Tom!" Elenna cried, her voice panicked. Tom looked back to see her lifting her chin. She was buried up to the chest!

We can't die like this. Drawing on every shred of strength he had left, Tom swallowed his rising terror and landed one final, mighty punch on the grille.

Crash!

It shattered against his fist. Brushing away the splintered glass,

Tom heaved himself out of the sand, the weight of it dragging down on his body. He was just able to see into the dim passage beyond.

Grunting, Tom turned to see the top of Elenna's head sink below

the surface. *No!* He tugged on the rope, but it didn't budge – as if the sand was pulling back, resisting his efforts. He felt suddenly sick.

Elenna will suffocate!

He pulled again with all the

magical might from his breastplate.
His heart hammered in his chest.
He forced himself to breathe slowly,
to think. Suddenly, he remembered
what he had told Elenna. *Stay still...*
He knew that if she struggled, the
quicksand would only swallow her
more quickly. *Of course!* The same
surely applied to him. Tom pulled
the rope once more, but this time he
hauled slowly and steadily. He felt it
move, and hope flared inside him.

Tom fed the rope through his
hands, bit by bit, his muscles
straining to keep up the slow effort,
while he ignored the way his worried
heart urged him to pull faster. The
top of Elenna's head emerged from

the sand, then her nose, her mouth. She took a ragged gasp of air, her eyes wide with terror. As soon as Elenna was within reach, Tom gripped her hand, and with one last tug, pulled her into the narrow glass tunnel.

"Are you all right?" Tom asked, as she caught her breath.

Elenna nodded. "Thanks to you," she said. "Now, let's see where this passage goes."

Tom took the lead, edging along the smooth glass on his hands and knees. Dusky blue light filtered into the cramped passage through the huge mass of crystal above them. The way led steadily upwards. Tired and

thirsty, Tom and Elenna clambered on
until the passage opened into a large
room. Unbending his aching muscles,
Tom took in his new surroundings –
cool and shady, with leaves and fruit

carved into the crystal ceiling, and spouts poking from the walls.

"It looks like some sort of bathing complex," Elenna said. "There must have been water here once."

"It's a shame there isn't now," Tom said, thinking of their water bottles. He led the way through the room into an antechamber with doors leading off to each side. Through an archway at the far end, Tom caught sight of a shadowy form holding what looked like an axe. He froze, his hand on the hilt of his sword. Following his gaze, Elenna drew her bow from her back and fitted an arrow.

Time to fight!

4

A CRYSTAL ARMY

Tom and Elenna charged through
the doorway, weapons raised. They
stopped dead, gaping. The archway
opened into an enormous shady hall,
filled with rows and rows of warriors.
But these weren't flesh and blood
fighters. Each person in uniform
was carved from crystal! There were
soldiers armed with swords and

maces, axes and spears. They stood
in ranks, shoulder to shoulder. But
they were all still and silent, eyes
blank. Had these once been living,
breathing fighters, now turned to
crystal? Or had this mute army been
carved from rock?

"I wonder why Zargon made
so many statues..." Elenna said,
taking in the strange sight. Her eyes
widened, and she shuddered. "Or
do you think they were once living
people?"

"I don't know," Tom said, rubbing
a sudden chill from his arms. "But
it's like a mausoleum. Let's get out
of here." He led the way back into
the lobby, and glancing through each

doorway, selected one that opened on to a narrow, winding staircase leading upwards. Maybe there were more clues up there.

The sunlight streaming through the crystal walls brightened steadily

as they climbed, making Tom's eyes smart. With the increasing light, the temperature rose, quickly becoming as stifling as the inside of a forge. Sweat made Tom's sword-grip slippery, and his head pounded with thirst. When he reached the top, a sudden flood of searing rays blinded him. He winced, narrowing his eyes against the glare, seeing that they were now in a long corridor with an arch in the wall at the far end. Beams of sunlight criss-crossed the passage in all directions, casting dancing rainbows across the floor.

"I can hardly see a thing!" Elenna said, her arm raised to protect her eyes from the dazzle.

Tom crept towards the opening, his back to the polished crystal and his sword lifted before him. As he neared the archway, the sound of muffled voices from inside made him catch his breath. He turned to Elenna, a finger to his lips, then tiptoed the last few steps. Keeping to the side of the opening, he pressed his nose to the thick glass of the wall. He could just make out the silhouettes of two figures moving about inside. With any luck it, would be Yara and Aroha. But he couldn't be sure...

Turning to Elenna, Tom tipped his head towards the doorway, and lifted his sword. Elenna slipped to his side. Brandishing their weapons, they both stepped through the arch.

"Well, if it isn't the Avantian Heroes…" said a familiar, scornful voice.

Yara!

Once Tom's eyes had adjusted, he saw that they were in a huge chamber. Graceful columns of carved glass held up a high, vaulted ceiling. Yara and the queen stood in the middle of the room, glaring back at them.

"That's right," Elenna snapped. "And these Avantians happen to have saved you Tangalans over and over since we left the palace!"

"Hush!" Aroha ordered, her eyes suddenly wide. "Listen!"

Tom's skin prickled as he heard a

strange buzzing drone. It seemed to be coming through the wall to the side of the queen, getting rapidly louder by the moment. A huge shadow fell over Yara and Aroha, as if a dark cloud had suddenly blotted out the sun.

"Run!" Tom cried. Too late.

The wall exploded with a crash. Everyone was showered with crystal shards as an enormous hornet-Beast buzzed into the room. The insect's vast body glistened blood-red, and its dual wings, striped black and yellow, moved in a noisy, clattering blur. Black, viscous liquid dripped from the creature's purple stinger, fizzing and smoking as it hit the floor, where it instantly burned through the crystal, dropping like acid into the room below.

Yara and Aroha backed away,

towards Tom and Elenna. Tom's hand fell to the red jewel in his belt – the jewel that allowed him to communicate with Beasts. Squaring his shoulders, he met the hornet's giant eyes.

Leave now, or I will defeat you, as I have defeated all the other Beasts of Vakunda, Tom told the huge insect as it hovered before him, wings clacking at a furious speed.

A grating, thrumming laugh like the chattering of a thousand locusts flooded Tom's mind. *I am Diprox*, the Beast told him. *No one has ever survived my wrath. You will flee, or you will die!* Angling her wings, Diprox swooped closer and curled her gleaming abdomen up to reveal the pointed sting in her tail. A dart of dark venom arced towards them.

"Behind me!" Tom cried, throwing his shield up as Yara, Elenna and the queen leapt for cover. Tom felt the thud of the venom hitting his shield, then an acrid smoke filled his nostrils as the wood smoked and fizzed.

Diprox laughed again, a hideous buzzing sound flooding Tom's mind. She flexed her body, angling her stinger once more. *Now you will all burn!* Her words rang through Tom's mind.

"Take cover!" he yelled to the others. He shoved his damaged shield behind a column. Then he leapt, putting the nearest glass pillar between himself and the Beast. Elenna and Yara did the same, but Aroha lunged towards Diprox, swinging her sword.

"No!" Tom cried. "The Beast means to kill us!" *What is she doing?*

Darting back in a flicker of wingbeats, Diprox dodged Aroha's blow. Her dark eyes flashed with triumph, and the Beast swooped on the queen. Aroha leapt aside, but Diprox followed, reaching out with forelegs lined with long, trembling hairs. At the end of each leg was a pincer, its jaws snapping greedily. With a sudden lunge, a pincer darted out and snatched the queen by the shoulders. Aroha cried out in fright and pain, her eyes pleading with Tom. But it was too late – the Beast

yanked Aroha from her feet. Tom leapt out in one last, desperate effort to save the queen.

"Drop her, now!" he shouted at Diprox. "Stay and fight!"

But with a scornful laugh, the Beast zipped away through the broken chamber wall and out into daylight. Tom heard Aroha's scream of fury fade slowly to nothing as she was carried high into the air, dangling in the giant hornet's grip.

A CRYSTAL COFFIN

"Do something!" Yara screamed at Tom and Elenna. She clambered over broken glass towards the gaping hole in the wall. "Aroha has the jewels!"

Tom and Elenna exchanged a glance, then hurried after Yara, who was lowering herself over the edge of the broken wall. They reached the opening to see the Tangalan warrior

drop down into a huge courtyard, with a drawbridge at one end. She set off running towards a high tower at the centre of the courtyard.

Diprox was dizzyingly high above them now. She seemed to be making her way towards a large window just below the tower's pointed roof, carrying Aroha with her.

"I'm going after Yara," Tom told Elenna. What choice did he have? He couldn't leave her to run rogue around the palace.

"I'm coming with you," his friend said.

The two of them peered down at the drop below. It would be easy to break an ankle – or worse – if they weren't careful. They exchanged a look, then nodded firmly.

Tom took a deep breath, bracing himself for the drop, then leapt through the gaping hole in the wall. The wind rushed past him as he plummeted towards the courtyard far below… He landed in a crouch, then leapt into a run with Elenna close behind. They reached the tower just as Yara ducked through its narrow doorway. Diving after her, Tom found a steep spiral staircase leading upwards. Each shallow step shone, and Tom's boots slipped again and again as he climbed.

As he neared the top, he suddenly heard the loud, unmistakeable buzz of Diprox's wingbeats. He peered through an arrow slit to see the Beast flying away from the tower. But her cargo had disappeared.

Where's Aroha?!

Tom clambered on, higher and

higher, until he heard the sounds of someone struggling or fighting, not far above – *Aroha!* He reached a doorway and leapt through, closely followed by Elenna. They found the queen, jaw clenched and face pale with anger, straining against a tight mesh of crystal net that held her fast. Yara stood to one side, watching Aroha struggle.

"We'll break you free!" Tom told the queen. He and Elenna sprang forwards, but Tom jerked to a halt when something wrapped around his body, as tight as a lasso. In a rapid, snaking movement, it pinned his arms to his sides, then strapped his legs together. He looked down to see

slender filaments of glass binding
themselves about him. He was
trapped in a crystal cocoon, just like
the queen's! Flexing his muscles,
he tried to break free, but the glass
lattice held him fast. Hearing an

angry cry from Elenna, Tom realised she had been trapped too. He struggled against his crystal bonds.

"Ooh, this is fun!" a voice said, as a figure stepped from a shadowy alcove. He came to stand between Tom and Aroha. *Zargon!* The wizard lifted his hand and sent another jet of web-like crystal towards Tom. Helpless fury burned inside him as the strands hit, wrapping so tightly around his body, he could barely move. It felt as though Tom was about to be buried alive in a crystal coffin! Yara still stood there, staring. She hadn't moved at all.

"Yara! Do something!" Tom cried.

But instead of bursting into action,

Yara just smiled. Then she stepped towards Zargon.

"You have done well, my friend," Zargon told her. "It took a little longer than we'd hoped, but you got there in the end. You shall be rewarded."

Tom felt a tidal wave of hot blood rising inside him.

"I knew you were after the jewels, Yara!" Elenna cried. "I just didn't think you'd actually be in league with Zargon!"

Yara's smile broadened. "Who's the stupid one now?"

Tom flexed his muscles against his cage again. This time, with fury pounding through his veins, he felt them give, just a little. He forced himself to relax and breathe evenly. *I'll break free...but not yet.*

"You will pay for your treachery, Yara," Aroha said from her cage. Tom had never heard such cold fury in the queen's voice. Or such hurt. "I will put you in the darkest cell in the palace. You will never see daylight again."

Yara shrugged. "You'll never see the palace again," she said breezily. "So, I think I'll be all right." Stepping towards the queen, Yara reached through the crystal mesh that held her, grabbed the pouch of gemstones from Aroha's belt, and tugged it free.

"No!" Aroha cried, as Yara dropped the pouch into the wizard's eager,

open palm.

"What about Rotu?" Aroha asked, after a moment. "Now you have the gemstones, you must set him free.

You promised."

Zargon shook his head. "I said I would free your nephew if you gave me the jewels," he said. "You didn't. I had to take them myself. The bargain is void. The prince is trapped in the highest tower of my palace. When all this is over, I might make him my squire." Aroha's face paled at that, and Zargon's smile broadened. "Or maybe I'll kill him. I haven't decided yet. But I do know that with the power of these jewels, Tangala and Avantia will be mine. Nothing can stop me now!"

AROHA'S ANGUISH

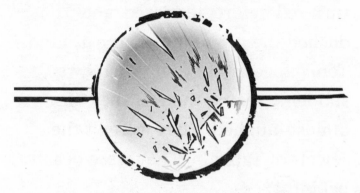

Zargon tipped the Jewels of Tangala from the pouch into his hand. As Tom watched, a crushing weight of hopelessness clutched his heart. *I've failed everyone*, he thought. *Rotu, the queen... All of Tangala and Avantia, too.*

The gemstones clinked as Zargon shifted them in his palm, staring

down at them, his forehead creased.
Tom saw the wizard's face slowly
turn red before he roared, and
dashed the gemstones to the ground.
Tom gaped as they clattered away,
suddenly seeing them clearly. He
almost laughed. They weren't the
Jewels of Tangala. They were beach
pebbles!

Zargon rounded on Yara, his fists
balled. "What are these worthless
objects? You fool!" he snarled.

Yara cringed away from the
wizard, then pointed at Aroha. "She
must have done something… I know
she had them. I've seen them."

Aroha's eyes were deep pools of
anger and pain, and Tom began

to realise he'd underestimated the
queen – had she planned this all
along? "I switched the jewels with

stones from the banks of the Crystal Sea," the queen said. "Rotu sent me a letter before his disappearance, warning me that you were behaving strangely. But because you have been a trusted member of our house for so long, I put his worries to the back of my mind. Then he was kidnapped, and nothing added up. Zargon was supposed to be magically imprisoned in Vakunda, so I knew someone must have taken Rotu to him. But still, I didn't want to believe one of my own warriors could be a traitor... It goes against everything we stand for! You are a disgrace to Tangala!"

"That's easy for you to say!" Yara screamed. "You have power over two whole kingdoms! You don't need Vakunda too! You should have given us the jewels at the start. You've ruined everything!"

Tom looked from the wizard, to Aroha, to Yara. Each had betrayed one of the others. He shared a grateful glance with Elenna from behind their crystal prisons. The two of them had gone through so much together – at least he knew they could always trust each other.

Yara suddenly drew her sword and leapt towards Aroha's cage, ready to strike the queen.

"Stop!" Zargon cried. "You can't kill her! She knows where the jewels are hidden." With Zargon's attention on Yara and the queen, Tom sensed his chance. He gave Elenna a small nod, to let her know to be ready. She nodded back. Then he took a deep breath, expanding his chest, flexing his muscles. He called on the power of his golden breastplate and the strength of heart of his chainmail combined. He felt his pulse quicken as he counted down the moments.

One, two, three...

SMASH!

His cage burst apart in a shower of glass. Turning, Tom swung his sword to break Elenna's prison. With two more steps, he strode towards Aroha and swiped again, freeing the queen. The crystal was

strong, but it shattered easily.

"You're going nowhere!" Zargon snapped, lifting his hand. A jet of crystal fibres shot from his fingertips. Tom ducked behind a column; in the same movement, he snatched up his damaged shield and hurled it into Zargon's face, while Elenna launched herself at Yara, bundling the traitor to the ground and knocking her sword from her grip.

As Elenna and Yara struggled, Zargon glared at Tom, one hand clamped over his bleeding nose, the other lifted, ready to cast a spell. Tom sprang forwards, grabbing the wizard's wrist and twisting his arm to wrench it up behind his back.

Over Zargon's shoulder, Tom caught Aroha's eye. "Leave these two to us," he told her. "Find Rotu." Reaching around Zargon's broad chest, Tom gripped his other arm.

"Thank you!" Aroha said and sprang away down the spiral stair. Zargon struggled to free himself. Tom grunted, using all the strength of his magical breastplate to keep the wizard from raising his hand and casting a spell. Suddenly, Zargon's body went heavy and slack. Caught off guard, Tom somehow managed to keep hold of the wizard, but then noticed his lips were moving.

He was muttering something...

No! Tom released his grip on Zargon's arm and clapped a hand over his mouth instead.

SPLAT!

The room darkened as something

black and oozing covered the outside
of one wall. The dark, viscous stuff
foamed and fizzed, dissolving the
crystal to reveal a patch of blue sky
and the hideous form of Diprox,
hovering in the air.

Zargon called the Beast!

Fumes filled Tom's lungs and burned his eyes, distracting him for long enough that Zargon slammed an elbow into his stomach, doubling him over, before breaking from his grip. Tom lunged after the wizard, but Zargon leapt straight through the damaged wall. He landed on Diprox's back, and flashed Tom an evil smile as the Beast turned and, with a terrible clacking of wings, flew away.

DIPROX'S REVENGE

Tom did not hesitate. He took three running steps and called on the power of his golden boots to leap from the tower, narrowly avoiding the Beast's deadly stinger as he reached for one of her legs. His stomach flipped as the hornet banked sharply, dragged down by

Tom's weight. With a hiss of fury,
she beat her wings harder, gaining
height; then she started thrashing,
trying to shake Tom off. His hands
slipped as he struggled to cling
on. He adjusted his grip but could

already feel himself sliding down
Diprox's leg.

He looked down between his
dangling feet. Far below, the
gleaming crystal flagstones of the
walled courtyard waited to break

his fall – and his bones. With a mighty kick, Diprox wrenched her leg free. Tom's stomach shot into his mouth as he plummeted towards the flagstones. He lifted his shield and called on the power of Arcta's eagle feather. With a sudden jolt, his fall slowed – but not enough. Bracing himself, Tom landed heavily, pain shooting up his legs, then stumbled into a run.

Ahead, Diprox flew onwards towards another tall tower with a turret, beyond the courtyard wall.

Zargon glared back at Tom from the Beast's back. The wizard lifted his hand, unleashing a blue bolt of magic which fizzed past Tom into an alcove, hitting a crystal statue of a soldier. The sculpture lurched into life, eyes blazing with light, and it lifted a spear. *Zap!* Zargon sent another crackling jet of magic towards a second glass statue. The soldier's eyes glowed bright, and it brandished a huge, spiked mace. "Kill him!" Zargon called down.

Tom stepped back, lifting his sword as the two statues bore down on him, their crystal weapons glinting and their eyes burning with a cold hungry light. *So, this is why the crystal soldiers are in the palace. They can be brought to life to protect it!*

Tom could see Zargon and Diprox

still heading towards the distant tower. *That must be where Rotu is!* But with the crystal soldiers closing in, Tom had no choice but to stay and fight.

He hunkered down, his weight on the balls of his feet, ready for action. The first soldier jabbed for Tom's chest with its spear. Tom leapt aside, but from the corner of his eyes he saw the other statue's mace swinging towards him. Ducking the spiked ball, Tom slashed for its owner's glass legs, but the soldier leapt back out of reach. Tom took a step back too, glancing between his two opponents. Both soldiers lunged at once. Tom smashed a spear-thrust

aside with his sword and raised
his shield to block the mace. The
force of the crystal ball sent him
staggering back, his arm throbbing
with pain.

This is hopeless, Tom thought. *I can't beat them by force. But maybe I can beat them with cunning.*

The statue with the spear jabbed for Tom's ribs. Instead of dodging back, Tom leapt towards the soldier, using his shield to slam the spear-tip away. As he had guessed, the second statue took the chance to strike, swinging its mace in a wide arc for Tom's head. Tom dropped into a crouch, ducking the blow, which whooshed over his head.

CRASH! The heavy spiked ball knocked the other soldier's head clean off its shoulders. The headless warrior toppled, shattering when it hit the ground. Tom sprang up and drove his sword through his remaining opponent's gut. The crystal soldier froze, dropping its spear. Its glowing eyes turned dark as it tumbled forwards, smashing to pieces at Tom's feet.

Wiping the sweat from his brow, Tom scanned the courtyard wall. Opposite the gatehouse to the moat, he spotted an archway that seemed to lead toward the distant tower. Snatching up the glass soldier's fallen spear, Tom broke into a run.

Speeding through the archway, Tom found himself in another wide courtyard with the high tower at the back, just as he'd hoped. He skidded to a halt. At the centre of the open space, Aroha and Rotu stood together, the open door of the tower just visible behind them. The prince looked thinner than Tom remembered him, and pale, but stood straight and tall at his aunt's side. The queen had rescued him!

But Diprox hovered above, with Zargon on her back.

"Tell me where you've hidden the jewels or you will both die," Zargon shouted. Tom saw Diprox angle her purple stinger towards Aroha and Rotu, black poison already dripping from its tip. Aroha glanced Tom's way, her eyebrows shooting up. Tom shook his head, warning her to be silent, and lifted the glass spear so she could see it. Then he began tiptoeing forward.

"If you kill me, you'll never find them," Aroha told Zargon. "I've hidden them far too well." Tom crept onwards, his eyes on Diprox's gleaming abdomen, as the queen stalled the wizard.

"No," Zargon cried. "It will just take me longer, that's all. And for that, you shall suffer. Get her!" he ordered the Beast. Diprox buzzed closer to the queen, her stinger throbbing. Tom drew back his arm and, calling on the strength of his golden breastplate, let the spear fly.

The crystal point drove deep into Diprox's scarlet body and the

spear lodged there. With a furious,
high-pitched buzzing drone, the
injured hornet started to writhe,

her wingbeats faltering, her body convulsing with pain. She jerked and spun in the air, bucking sharply, throwing Zargon from her back. The wizard's body slammed into the courtyard wall, slid down to the floor, and lay still.

Diprox went on thrashing and jerking, her hideous buzzing now so high and loud, Tom had to cover his ears. She plummeted, landing on her back. With her wings still flapping helplessly and her legs wriggling, Diprox turned circles on the slippery floor. A jet of black acid shot from her stinger. Aroha yanked Rotu out of range as the acid sprayed in an arc, fizzing and hissing as it hit crystal flagstones and walls. A great spurt covered the base of the tower at the back of the courtyard, sizzling as it ate into the glass.

Diprox's horrible buzzing finally stopped. Her thrashing movements slowed and her twitching legs fell still. Tom let out a long sigh, but then heard the sound of creaking and cracking... The ground began to shake. Glancing across the courtyard, Tom saw the tower Diprox had sprayed with acid listing, chunks of crystal toppling from its walls as it crumbled.

"Run!" he shouted, sprinting away as a massive lump of glass plummeted towards him. Rotu and

Aroha raced to his side. Together, they ran for their lives, dodging falling masonry as they pounded over the flagstones.

With terrible splintering crashes ringing out behind him, Tom led Rotu and Aroha back towards the first courtyard, heading for the drawbridge. But as he sped through the archway, a line of crystal soldiers blocked his way, each with furious blazing eyes, and each brandishing a glinting weapon.

JUST REWARDS

We don't have time for this! Tom
thought. The sound of crystal
smashing apart behind him was
almost deafening. The ground
juddered, and cracks sped along the
courtyard walls. *The whole palace
is breaking apart.* Tom's thoughts
flashed to Elenna. He'd left her
in the tower where they'd found

Aroha, fighting Yara… All he could do was hope she'd got out.

"Charge!" Tom shouted, lifting his sword. Aroha let out a battle cry.

"I'm with you!" Rotu shouted. Tom, Aroha and Rotu all lunged together.

CRASH! Tom hacked a soldier in two with a double-handed strike to the gut.

SMASH! Aroha chopped the head off another.

THUD! Rotu landed a roundhouse kick in the chest of a third.

Without looking back, all three of them sprinted past the rest of the soldiers towards the gatehouse. Tom could already see a network of fractures spreading through the crystal structure. Glancing back, he felt his heart give a leap. The remaining glass soldiers were hot on their trail, gaining fast.

Tom sped through the gatehouse, feeling a rush of hope when he saw the drawbridge had lowered to span the moat. *Maybe Elenna did escape – and we can too!* But then his hope evaporated as he noticed a huge crack, right across the middle of it, cleaving it in two. *It's broken!*

"Tom! We have to go! Now!"

Aroha cried. A dark shadow fell across him – the pointed shadow of the top of the tower, plummeting their way.

"Hold tight!" Tom told Aroha and Rotu, linking an arm through each of theirs. Then, calling on the power of his golden boots, he leapt, taking them with him over the broken bridge and the deadly quicksand as the tower smashed down behind them, with a deafening crash.

BOOF! They landed together in a tangled heap on the far bank of the moat. Scrambling up, Tom turned to see Zargon's whole palace tumbling into ruins with a din of splintering crunches and earth-shaking booms.

Finally, the noise subsided, leaving
only a twinkling haze of crystal dust
hanging in the air.

"Well, that's the last of Zargon's
army of statues!" Tom said. "Surely
nothing could survive…" Tom's heart

clenched as ice-cold horror washed over him. "Elenna!" he cried.

"You called?" a cheerful voice said from behind him. Tom sagged, dizzy with relief, and turned to see Elenna holding one end of a rope, the other end tied tightly about Yara's wrists.

"How did you escape?" he asked.

"When everything started to break apart, I thought we'd better get out," Elenna said. Yara stood scowling darkly at her feet. "We made it across the drawbridge just before it broke. Although I'm not sure why I bothered to bring Yara! She's done nothing but moan."

"She's lucky to be alive," Aroha said, clapping a hand down on

Tom's shoulder. Thinking the queen meant to thank him for his efforts, Tom felt a warm blush rise to his cheeks.

"It was no more than my duty," he started. But then he noticed Aroha tugging off one of her boots. She tipped the boot up and shook four glittering gemstones into her palm.

"The Jewels of Tangala! You had them the whole time," Elenna said. Aroha nodded.

"I'm sorry I had to keep you both in the dark for so long," she said. "But I needed to gain Yara's trust in order to get close to Zargon." She selected a clear, colourless gem, very like the crystal of Zargon's

fallen palace, and held it up to
the light. For a moment, nothing
happened. Then Tom noticed the
motes of crystal dust still hanging
in the air streaming towards the
gemstone, vanishing into it. The
rest of the fallen crystal structure
shimmered and blurred, forming a
glittering, swirling diamond cloud,
shot through with rainbow light.
Then it too flowed into the stone
in Aroha's hand, faster and faster,
until everything was gone. The
stone flared brightly for a moment,
a silver star caught between the
queen's fingers, then finally went
dark.

Tom shook his head, suddenly

groggy, as if waking from a dream. He blinked and refocussed his eyes to find himself standing on an island of fresh green grass, studded with flowers, and buzzing with perfectly normal-sized insects.

"It's over!" Tom said, grinning. "We did it!" He noticed Elenna frowning as she swept her gaze over the meadow.

"Yes. But where's Zargon?" she said. "Surely he didn't get sucked up by the jewel too?"

Aroha closed her fingers over the gemstones. "Frankly, I don't care. As long as I never have to set eyes on him again," she said. Tom couldn't help agreeing, but Elenna's words

had stirred a nagging doubt in his gut. *Evil Wizards do have a habit of reappearing when you least expect them...*

"Speaking of Zargon," Rotu said, "what are you going to do with his accomplice?" The prince jerked a thumb towards Yara, who scowled back at him.

"I can think of any number of suitable punishments," Aroha said, gazing thoughtfully at their prisoner. "Grashkor's Prison Island, for instance?"

Yara paled. "No!" she cried. "Anything but that!"

"All right," Aroha said. "I think it should be down to Rotu to pass the punishment, once we've all returned home."

Rotu grinned. "That sounds fair," he said. "Actually, there is a statue of me I was hoping to commission. One that will require lots of stones brought from the quarry. Yara's strong – she'll be perfect for the job. And it will only take about twenty years or so... But first, I'll want to arrange a feast to honour my aunt and my two other brave rescuers." He smiled warmly at Tom and Elenna. "Without you, I'd still be imprisoned in that tower!"

Tom and Elenna shared a smile as Aroha and Rotu linked arms and set off over the grass. The Quest to Vakunda had almost cost both of them their lives. But seeing Rotu at his aunt's side once more, and Aroha safe to return to King Hugo and their baby son, made it all worthwhile.

Another villain vanquished...another Quest successfully completed!

THE END

1

CONGRATULATIONS, YOU HAVE COMPLETED THIS QUEST!

At the end of each chapter you were awarded a special gold coin.
The QUEST in this book was worth an amazing 8 coins.

Look at the Beast Quest totem picture opposite to see how far you've come in your journey to become

MASTER OF THE BEASTS.

The more books you read, the more coins you will collect!

Do you want your own
Beast Quest Totem?

1. Cut out and collect the coin below
2. Go to the Beast Quest website
3. Download and print out your totem
4. Add your coin to the totem

www.beastquest.co.uk

READ THE BOOKS, COLLECT THE COINS!
EARN COINS FOR EVERY CHAPTER YOU READ!

550+ COINS
MASTER OF
THE BEASTS

410 COINS
HERO

350 COINS
WARRIOR

230 COINS
KNIGHT

180 COINS
SQUIRE

44 COINS
PAGE

8 COINS
APPRENTICE

READ ALL THE BOOKS IN SERIES 25:
THE PRISON KINGDOM!

Don't miss the first book in this series: AKORTA, THE ALL-SEEING APE!

Read on for a sneak peek...

WOUNDED WARRIOR

Tom sat on a low stone wall in Daltec's apothecary garden, the sun on his back and the sweet scent of herbs and flowers all around him.

Nearby, Daltec picked tiny blue leaves from a woody shrub and dropped them into a pouch at his belt. "That should be enough to fix Captain Harkman's back," he said, straightening up.

A little further along the flowerbed, Elenna leaned towards a purple rose with velvety-looking petals. "These flowers smell amazing!" she said, closing her eyes and taking a long sniff. "Almost like...biscuits baking."

"Careful!" Daltec said. "That's a Gorgonian rose."

Elenna took another sniff, but with a jolt of horror Tom saw the rose's petals peel apart, revealing white, human-like teeth. "Look out!" he cried, as Elenna leapt back with a yelp.

"I warned you..." Daltec said, barely stifling a grin as Elenna eyed the rose crossly. It had settled back into place as if nothing had happened.

Tom got to his feet, glancing warily at the tidy rows of plants all around him. Suddenly, an alarm horn blared from the direction of the palace gate.

Tom frowned. "That sounds like trouble!"

He set off at a run, with Elenna and Daltec close behind him. They sped through the palace gardens, under the stone archway and into the main courtyard. Tom skidded to a stop just as a huge white horse cantered through the palace gates. The creature's heaving sides were flecked with foam. Its rider, a tall knight in full armour, pulled the animal to a halt, then slid from the

saddle. He swayed, lifting a hand as if about to speak, then collapsed to the cobbles with a clatter.

Tom leapt to the fallen warrior's side. He knelt and gently eased off the knight's helmet. Wisps of auburn hair clung to a woman's face, damp with sweat. Her skin looked sunburnt, and a long cut, crusted with dried blood, sliced across one of her cheekbones. Her eyes fluttered open, deep blue, but unfocussed. "Aroha…" she croaked, before slipping back into unconsciousness.

Tom stood at the foot of the wounded soldier's bed, watching as Daltec applied a poultice to the cut on the woman's face. Her armour had been removed, but she had not yet stirred. Apart from the patient's laboured breathing, the infirmary was silent. The quiet was soon broken by the sound of hurrying feet.

"Yara!" cried Queen Aroha, as she burst into the room.

Crossing quickly to the soldier's bedside, the queen took the woman's sunburnt hand in her own. "Yara is one of my most trusted warriors in Tangala," she said, frowning. "She's the personal guard of my nephew, Rotu. Something terrible must have happened for her to come all this way…"

Daltec nodded gravely. "Her injuries are not life-threatening, but it seems she has ridden for days without rest. The journey has taken its toll."

The woman let out a groan, her face twisting.

"Yara?" Aroha said softly. The warrior's eyes opened. She seemed to flinch back from Aroha's gaze.

"You're in the City," Aroha told her. "You're safe."

Yara shook her head, her forehead creased with anguish. "I'm so sorry, Your Majesty," she said. "I have failed you. Rotu has been kidnapped."

Tom felt a jolt of alarm. He knew the young prince well, and though they had not always seen eye to eye, it was grave news to hear he was in danger.

Aroha gasped. "Kidnapped? By whom?"

"By Zargon, of Vakunda," Yara croaked.

The queen's face drained of colour. "Impossible…" she breathed.

"Who is Zargon?" Tom asked. He had rarely seen the queen look so troubled.

Aroha closed her eyes for a moment. "Zargon was the last wizard of Tangala," she said finally. "More than five hundred years ago, he stole the four Jewels of Tangala and used them to enchant a desert region to the south, called Vakunda. He created his own kingdom there with four distinct realms – bountiful forests, mountains of gold, a great river and a fertile island paradise

where he built a home. Each realm
was guarded by a Beast."

Tom's pulse quickened at the
mention of Beasts. "Are they still
there?" he asked.

Queen Aroha nodded. "I believe so."

Read
AKORTA, THE ALL-SEEING APE
to find out what happens next!